P9-CAJ-526

The King and the Whirlybird

By Mabel Watts

Pictures by Harold Berson

Parents' Magazine Press · New York

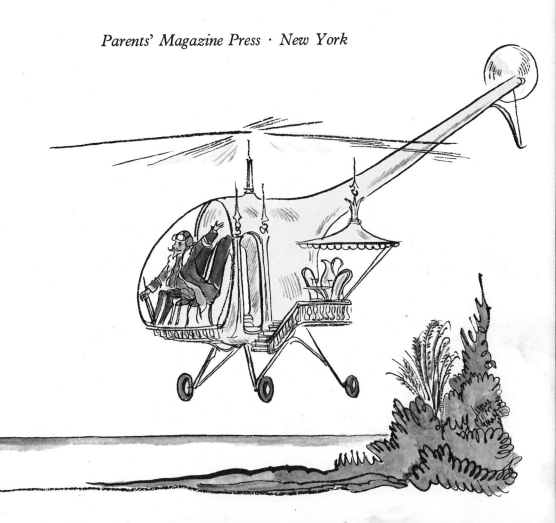

Text Copyright © 1969 by Mabel Watts
Illustrations Copyright © 1969 by Harold Berson
All rights reserved
Printed in the United States of America
Standard Book Numbers: Trade 8193-0289-9, Library 8193-0290-2
Library of Congress Catalog Card Number: 69-12605

To Bruce and Brian, two real high flyers.

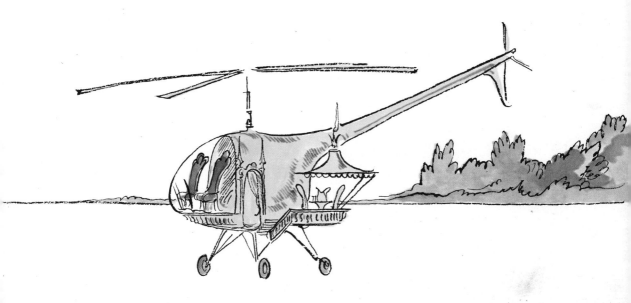

ONCE THERE WAS a King who owned a wonderful kind of flying machine called a whirlybird.

He had a pilot who could fly it, by the name of Joe.

But the King would not fly.

The whirlybird had its very own hangar. And its very own whirly-port.

But the King would have nothing to do with any of them.

"Flying is for the birds," he said. "And I'm not a bird!"

"There are other ways to travel," said His Majesty the King.

And he traveled quite a lot.

The King once had to travel to a coronation. He had to see his cousin get most gloriously crowned.

"Fetch the royal coach!" roared the King.

"The ancient old coach with the wobbly old wheels?" asked Joe the Pilot, who was also Joe the Coachman.

"That's the one," said the King.

"The coach that goes careening down the hills?" asked Joe. "The coach that throws you down into a heap upon the floor?"

"You know perfectly well which one I mean!" said the King.

"The newest way to travel is by whirlybird," said Joe. "It's the modern way for going round about!"

"Flying is for the birds," said the King. "And I'm NOT a bird!"

And he rode in the royal coach to the coronation.

"There are other ways to travel," said His Majesty the King.
And he traveled quite a lot.

Every day Joe showed the King all the wonderful things the whirly-bird could do.

He spun it right straight up in the air, with its engines buzzing, and its rotors turning.

He spun it right straight down, the same way.

He made it shuttle sideways. And backwards. And full speed ahead.

He made it hover above the King, and waggle its tail . . . like a hummingbird over a honeysuckle bush.

"There's very little traffic in the air," said Joe. "Besides, it would do Your Majesty good to try something new!"

But the King would not fly. He was a regular old king-in-the-mud!

"Flying is for the birds," he said. "NOT for people!

"There are other ways to travel," said His Majesty the King.

And he traveled quite a lot.

The King once had to travel to a little village square. He had to lay a cornerstone so that a school could be built.

"Fetch the royal stallion!" roared the King.

"The big black stallion that will not lift his feet, no matter what?" asked Joe the Pilot, who was also Joe the Stableboy.

"That's the one!" said the King.

"The wild black stallion that bumps you up and down and gives you indigestion?" asked Joe.

"You know perfectly well which one I mean," said the King.

"The quickest way to travel is by air," said Joe. "And nothing in the world is quite as nice!"

"Flying is for the birds," said the King. "It's too fast and fancy for me!"

And he rode the royal stallion to the little village square.

"There are other ways to travel," said His Majesty the King.

And he was *always* on the go!

The King once had to travel to a park in a faraway city to open a playground for the children.

"Fetch the royal train!" roared the King.

"The rattly old train with the smoky old engine?" asked Joe the Pilot, who was also Joe the Train Engineer.

"That's the one," said the King.

"The mean old train that blows cinders all over your robes every time it goes around a bend?" asked Joe.

"That's the one," said the King.

"The crawly old train that stops at all the crossings, and is always, always late?" asked Joe.

"You know very well which train I mean," said the King.

"You'd get a better view from the whirlybird," said Joe. "The lark gets a much better view than the worm!"

"The whirlybird looks like a flying windmill," said the King. "And what would my people think if they saw their King flying around in a windmill?"

"They would think you were adventurous," said Joe. "And most up-to-date."

The King rather liked the idea of being adventurous and up-to-date. He wanted to know the feel of riding in a whirlybird. And how *did* the world look from up above? The King really wanted to know— but not that much. "Some other day," he said. "But not today!"

And he rode the royal railway to the park in the city.

"There are other ways to travel," said His Majesty the King.
And he traveled quite a lot.

One day the King had to travel to the waterfront. He had to launch a steamship that was waiting at the dock.

"Fetch the royal jeep!" roared the King.

"The little brown jeep that looks like a beetlebug?" asked Joe the Pilot, who was also Joe the Royal Chauffeur.

"That's the one," said the King.

"The jeep that jumps the rocks and ditches, and blows your hat off?" asked Joe.

"You know very well which jeep I mean," said the King.

"The whirlybird rides smooth as cream," said Joe. "It's the very best invention in this go-ahead old world!"

"As I said before," replied the King, "I'm not a bird!"

And he rode the royal jeep to the busy waterfront.

"There are other ways to travel," said His Majesty the King.

And he traveled quite a lot.

One day the King traveled to the mountains to gather rocks for his rock collection. He went on foot because it was a nice sunny day and he needed the exercise.

He went with Joe the Pilot, who was also Joe the Royal Companion.

And then it happened.

The King reached for a rock with beautiful gold flecks in it. He simply had to have that rock. His heart was set on it.

But the King reached out too far....

He missed his footing, and down he went over a ledge, in a shower of stones.

Down went the King, slipping and sliding, with his hat going one way and his gold-buckled shoes going another. And there was nothing to stop him . . . nothing at all . . . nothing at all until he reached the bottom!

The King looked up at the towering cliffs, so awfully high, and so fearfully steep. "Only a fly could climb out of here," roared the King. "And I'm not a fly!"

"All we need is a rope," Joe the Pilot called down. "We'll soon get you out with a rope!"

Joe got in touch with the palace on his walkie-talkie. "Send the longest, toughest rope you can find!" he said.

At the bottom of the canyon the King sucked on a lemon drop and waited.

And after a while the rope arrived.

AND
THEN
IT
WAS
JUST
A
LITTLE
TINY
BIT
TOO
SHORT!

The King twitched with impatience. "Try something else," he said. "And hurry!"

The King's men sent down a fallen tree. It went crashing down into the canyon and scared the King half to death. "And what am I supposed to do with *that?*" he asked.

"You stand the tree against the canyon wall," said the King's men. "And up you climb."

"All by myself?" said the King. "Don't be silly!"

"We could fill the canyon full of water and *float* you up!" said the King's men. "How's that for an idea?"

"Too wet," said the King. "Much too wet!"

"We could make ourselves into a sort of chain," said the King's men. "And you could climb up over our backs and shoulders."

"It just wouldn't work," said the King. "And someone might get hurt."

"Well," said Joe. "What is your wish?"

"Fetch the royal whirlybird!" roared the King.

"The whirlybird that has its very own hangar, and its very own whirlyport?" asked Joe the Pilot.

"That's the one!" said the King.

"The whirlybird that will go right straight up? And right straight down?" asked Joe. "And sideways? And backwards? And full speed ahead?"

"You know very well which one I mean!" said the King.

"That's all I wanted to know!" said Joe.

And away he went to fetch the royal whirlybird.

"Help has come," cried the King, when he heard its buzzing. "The *right* sort of help!"

The whirlybird floated down into the canyon, with its engines humming and its rotors turning.

Joe lowered the rope ladder. It wiggled and wobbled in the breeze. And up climbed the King—up the strong rope steps to safety.

The King looked down at the beautiful view. "The royal stallion couldn't have saved me," he said as he traveled through the sky for the very first time. "Nor the royal coach. Nor the royal train. Nor the royal jeep—"

"But the whirlybird could do it. And it DID!" laughed Joe.

The King was now an up-to-date monarch. He was most adventurous and no longer a king-in-the-mud.

Joe made the whirlybird hover over the palace, like a puppet on a string. He made it really whirl, like a windmill with wings.

And the King was delighted. "Flying is for the birds," he said. "And it's great for people, too. . . .

"There are many ways to travel," said His Majesty the King. "And the whirlybird is best!"